FLATLAND

The story of Owuza Flatlander

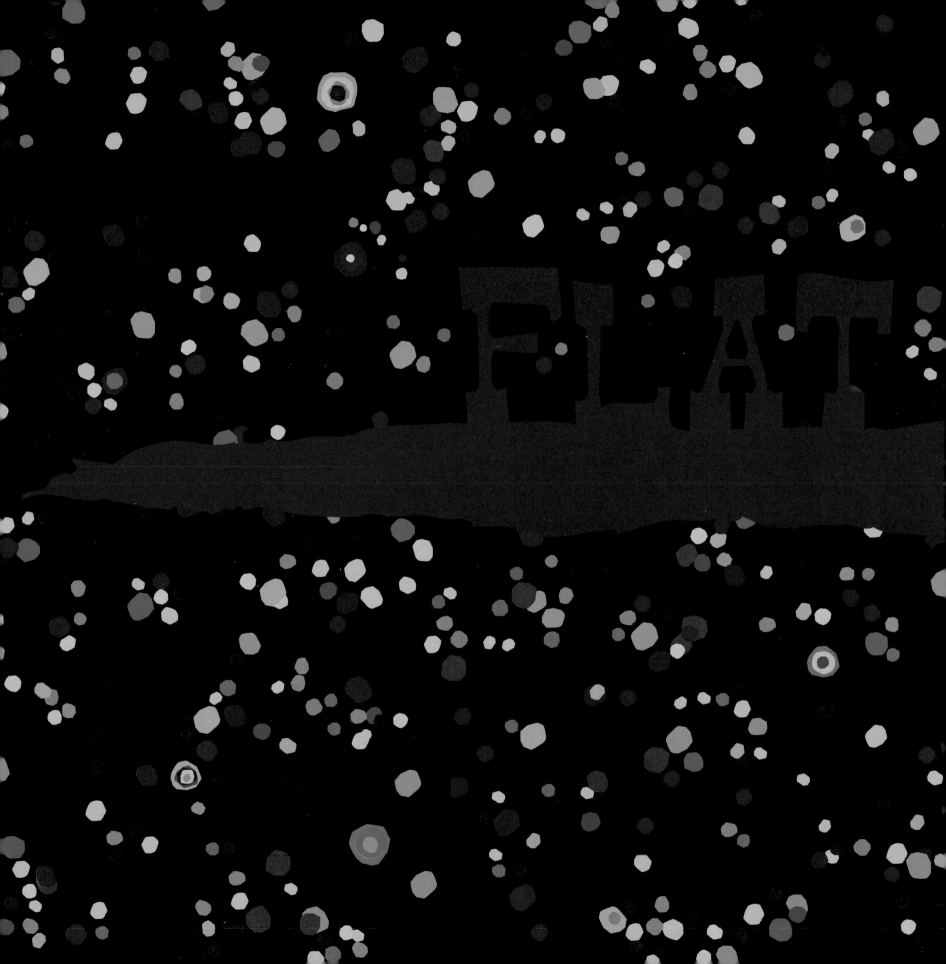

LAND

David Sayre & Rebecca Emberley

two little birds

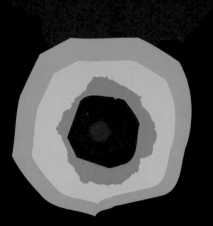

When Owuza arrived in Flatland
he was no more than a speck.

Flatland was wild and dark

jumbly and LOUD.

Owuza had to stretch
and grow and learn.

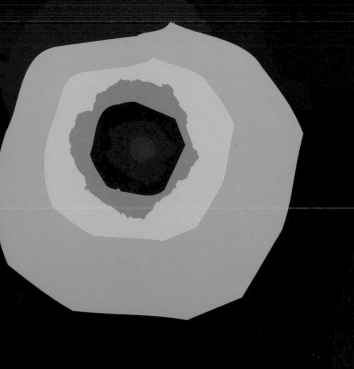

He had to learn
to see the new sights,

to hear the new sounds

and to sniff the new smells.

Everything was exciting
and sometimes scary.

Owuza wanted to share
all the new things
he was learning
and feeling.

So he set off to wander Flatland
and found lots of friends.

Everyone had something
to share,
stories to be told,
songs to be sung.

They were all happy
together in this wild new
place, and Owuza soon
forgot the time before
he came to Flatland.

Owuza was bursting
with feelings and ideas.

As he shared them, they
began to take root and grow.

Sharing his ideas
made him feel free
to be more than he was.

Together
the Flatlanders
BUILT,

they created,

they made beautiful things.

They learned how to
HELP and to HEAL

and to share lots of LOVE.

This was life on Flatland.

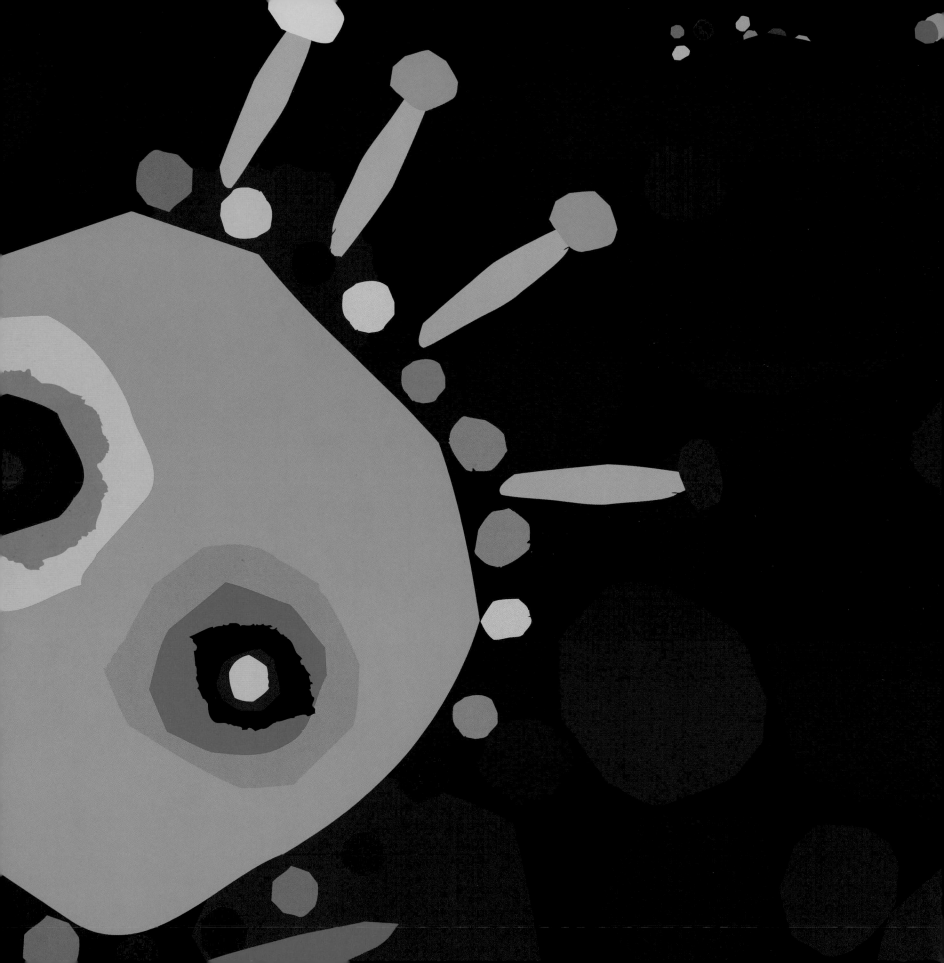

Owuza loved this life with his friends.

Sometimes he wondered, if this was here,
was there something else there?

He was content learning and sharing life
on Flatland, so he did not wonder too often.

Still, Flatland had edges and endings.

Finally – they reached out to each other, and

In all that they shared,

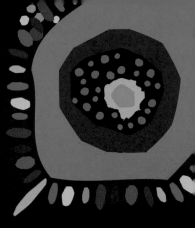

They turned Flatland upside down,
calling out, looking here,
looking there.
But, no Owuza.

They were confused.

If he was not there,
where was he?

One day the Flatlanders awoke
and Owuza was not there.

he was with them always.

there, in the center of them all, was Owuza.

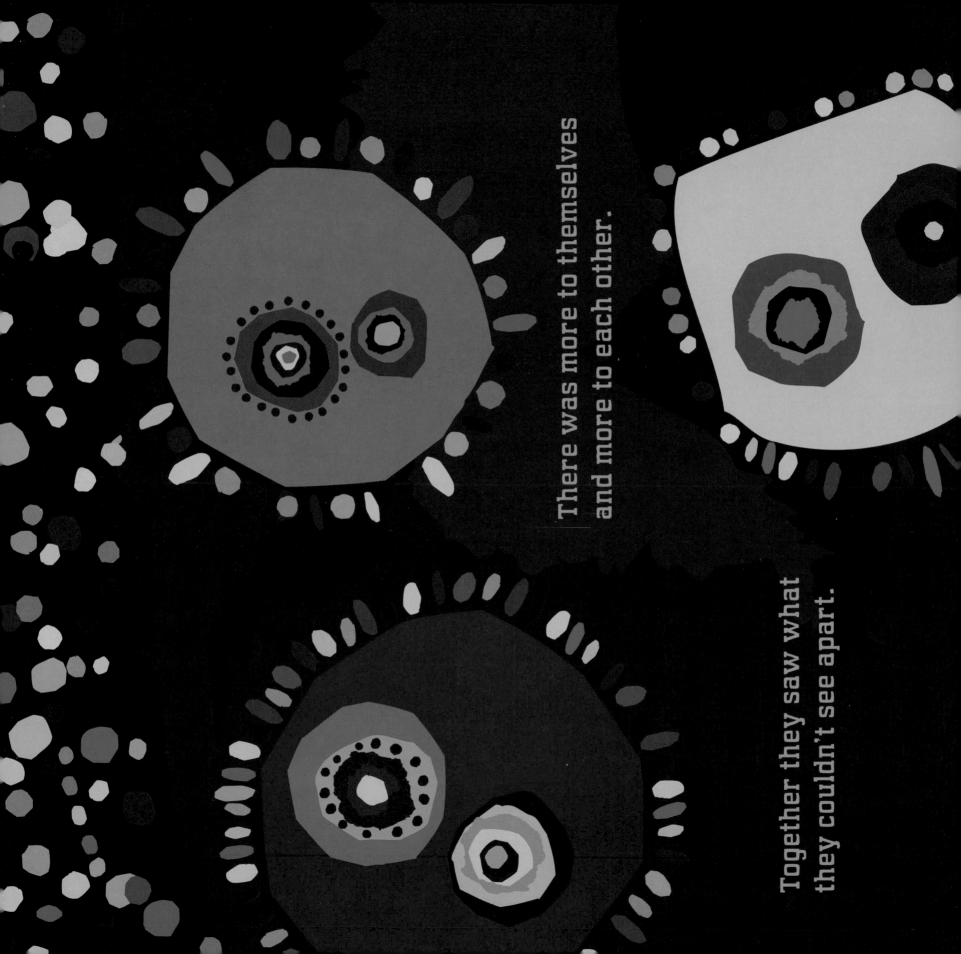

There was more to themselves
and more to each other.

Together they saw what
they couldn't see apart.

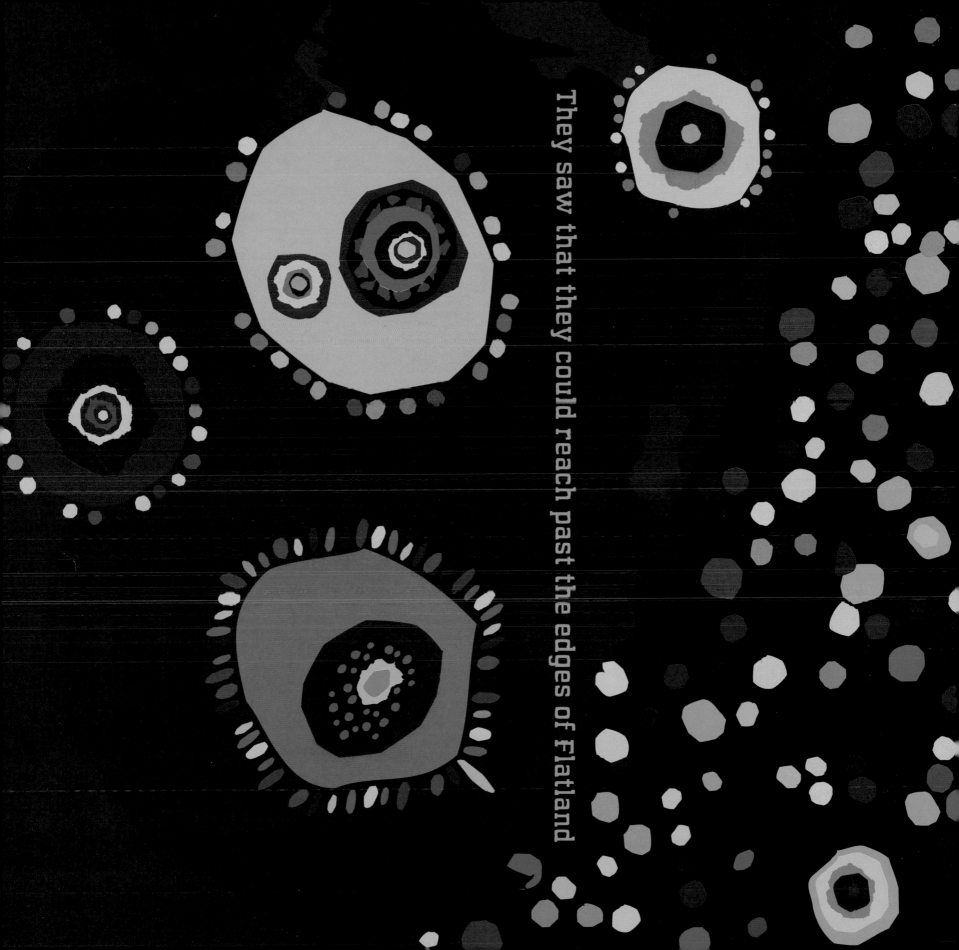

They saw that they could reach past the edges of Flatland

and they could leave those endings behind.

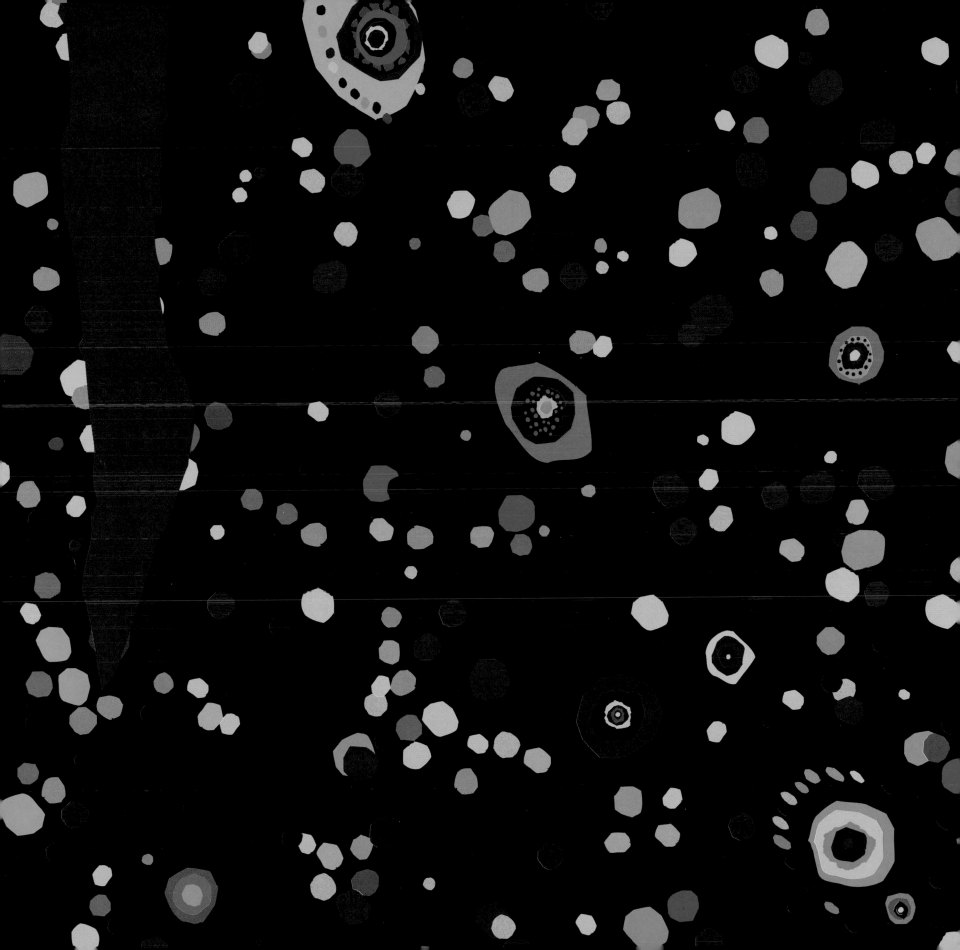

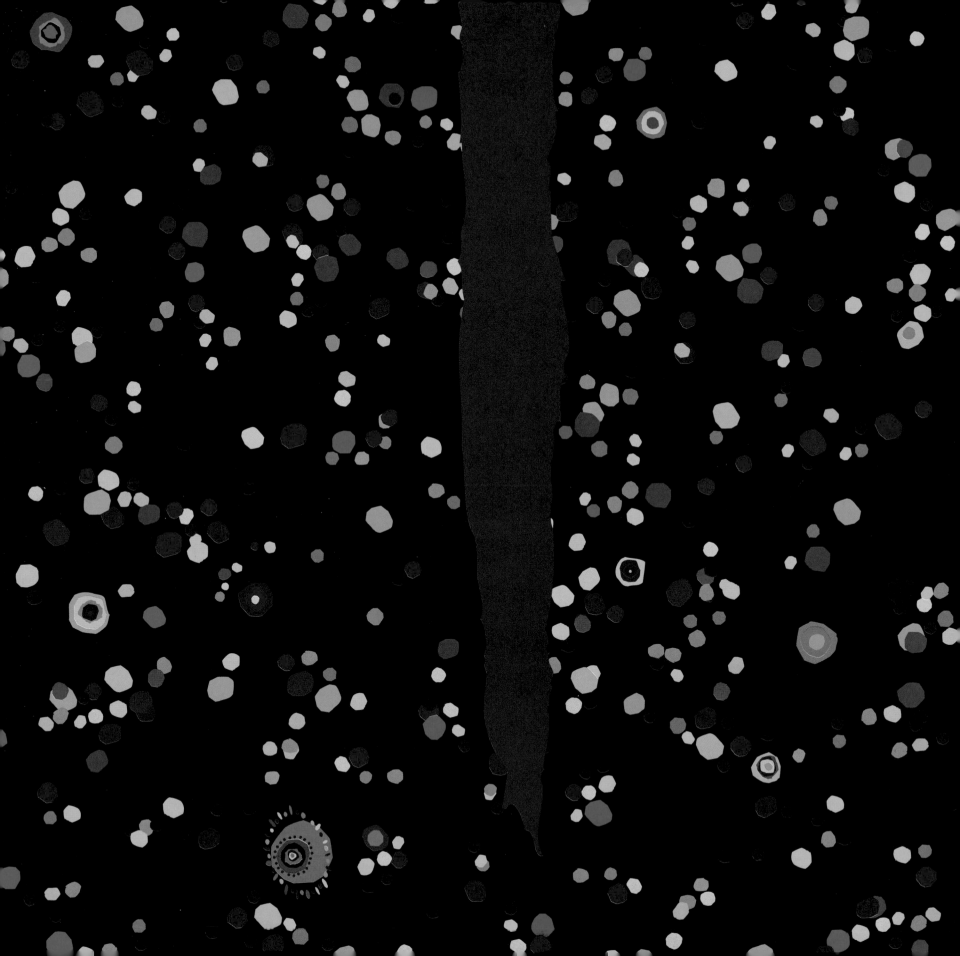

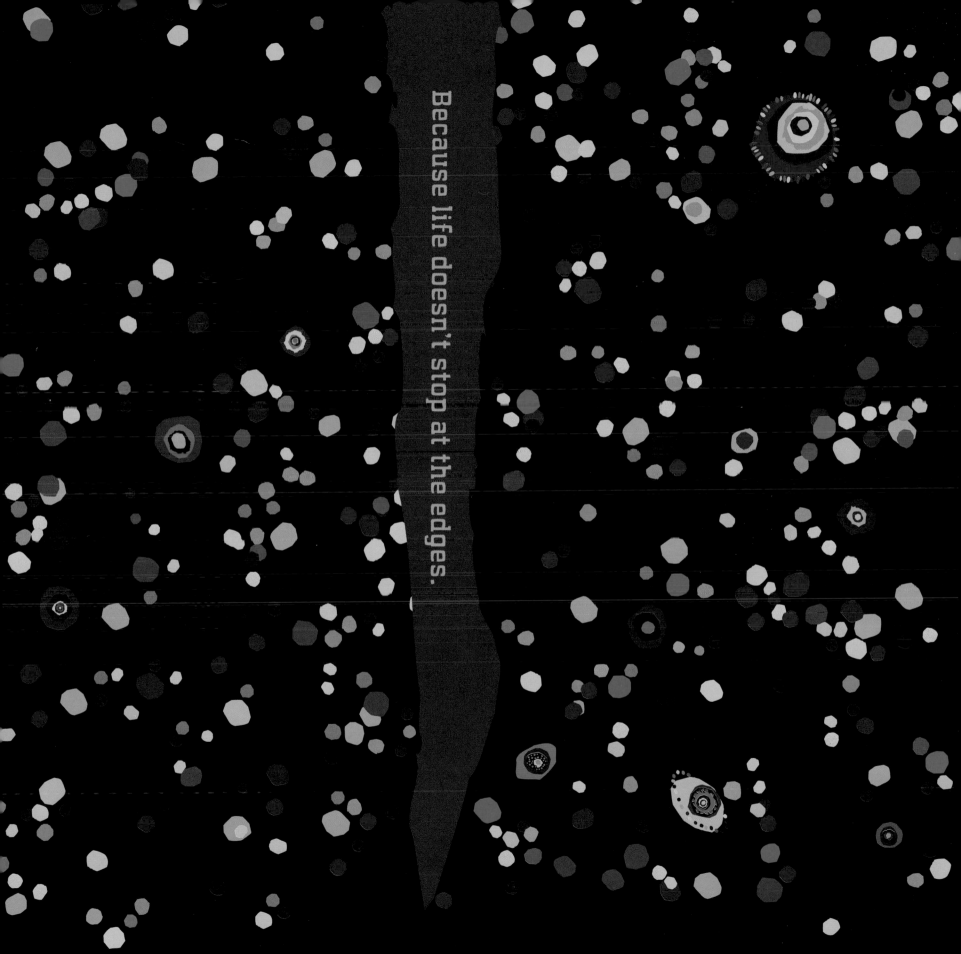

Because life doesn't stop at the edges.

David Sayre is an author and an engineer, known for his work in the sciences of communication and energy efficiency and their reduction of entropy. He is also a father. The story of Owuza Flatlander grew out of his family's search for comfort and understanding following the loss of his daughter. His hope is to share that understanding with children and adults. David lives in Bennington, Vermont with his wife. Flatland is David's first book for children.

You can read more about David and his writings at:
www.davidsayre.com

Rebecca Emberley is a picture book author and illustrator. She was drawn to illustrate the story of Flatland as it echoed her own beliefs and experience. Each illustration in the book is created from the elements on the title page's depiction of the universe. She was inspired by the art of ancient indigenous cultures around the world. Rebecca lives in Kittery, Maine with her husband, two cats and five chickens.

You can read more about Rebecca and her work at:
www.rebeccaemberley.com

©2013 David Sayre, Rebecca Emberley
Jacket Design © 2013 Rebecca Emberley

First edition April 2014
Two Little Birds Books
www.twolittlebirdsbooks.com

Libray of Congress Cataloging-in-Publication Data

ISBN 978-0-9912935-0-6
1. Picture book.
2. Universe. String Theory. Loss. Entropy. Grief. Explore.
Seven Evidences. Pre-K – Adult

Distributed by AMMO Books
www.ammobooks.com

Print production by TWP, Malaysia